tumbleweed press

Old Timers – The One That Got Away
ISBN 0-9683303-1-2
Tumbleweed Press, 401 Magnetic Drive,
Unit 11, Downsview, Ontario, M3J 3H9
www.tumbleweed-press.com
Book Design: Julian Dormon Art & Design

OLD TIMERS

THE ONE THAT GOT AWAY!

©COPYRIGHT 1998

tumbleweed press

Thompson-Nicola Regional District
Library System
300-465 VICTORIA STREET
KAMLOOPS, BC   V2C 2A9

We went to visit Pop one day

With pictures of our past

Cause he's been forgetting lots of things

So just in case he asked

We brought him shots of Grandma

And that one of Uncle Phil

With his children: Sara, Jacob

And the youngest one, named Will

And we had The one of us with him

From when we were all young

We spenT The summer aT The lake

And Pop had so much fun

"You went skiing and Tried sailing"

As my mother did remind

"But fishing was The favourite

Of all The Things you Tried"

"Remember how you almost caught

'The one That goT away'

And The size you said iT was

And how heavy iT had weighed"

But my Papa Joe just stared at her

As if it was a chore

Then he looked up at me and asked

"Have I been here before?"

"We came To say hello To him"

My moTher did explain

"Because he has a Kind of sickness

ThaT will boTher wiTh his brain"

She said iT was "Old Timers"

Or so I ThoughT I heard

BuT iT was called Al-z-heimer's

A very hard-To-pronounce word

So I Tried To understand it

That my Papa Joe was ill

With a problem That would hurt his mind

With no cure from a pill

I decided I was lucky

To have known my Pop so long

And I knew That he was healThy

Cause his body was sTill sTrong

Then I hugged my Pop real TighT

And kissed him on The cheek

And I knew ThaT I would love him

Every minuTe, every week

As long as I had memories

Of all The Times we shared

Then I would noT feel so bad

And I could noT be so scared

Because I got To love my Grandfather

For all Ten years of my life

And one day I'll Tell his sTories

To my children and my wife

And I'll be sure To share The one abouT

'The One ThaT GoT Away'

And I would caTch iT just for him

on my nexT fishing day

TO WHAT WAS, WHAT IS AND WILL FOREVER STAY ALIVE IN MY THOUGHTS, NO MATTER HOW TIME CHANGES THINGS.

Thank you for my memories – Mom and Dad, Ora, Izzy, Grandma and Pop, Bubbie, Auntie Rise and Harry, Ayelet, Rebecca and Sari, Auntie Shelly and Michael, Jeremy, Jonathan and Jodi, Auntie Reesa and David, Ari, Sury, Kari and Lauren, Melanie and Jonnie, Jen L, Jen C, Pam, Shauna, Ron, and all my friends, associates and acquaintances, and, of course, all my students: past, present and future who inspire me daily.

Tumbleweed thanks:
Andrea Olson, Linda LeDuc, Rod Wilson, Bill Dillane, Sylvia Watts, Jennifer Cairns, Victoria Boon, David Matlow, Brian Kimmel and Helen Walsh for their advice, friendship and support.

Noa, Erica and Julian for their passion and talent.